P9-ARD-793

HAVERHILL
PUBLIC LIBRARY

ANGRY BIRDS™

STELLA AND THE HUNT FOR THE JADE EGG

ANGRY BIRDS™

STELLA AND THE HUNT FOR THE JADE EGG

INSIGHT KIDS

San Rafael, California

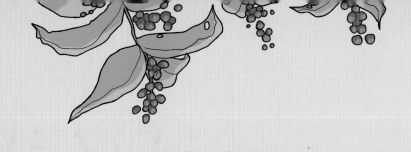

MEET THE CHARACTERS

THE ANGRY BIRDS ARE A FLOCK OF BIRDS WHO LIVE ON PIGGY ISLAND.
THEY MUST DEFEND THEMSELVES AGAINST THE BAD PIGGIES,
WHO ARE ALWAYS ATTEMPTING TO STEAL THEIR LAST THREE EGGS.

STARRING!

BUBBLES

is small and cute but doesn't talk very much.
He expands like a balloon to get what he wants.

STELLA

is independent and stubborn.
She doesn't like to be given orders.

MATILDA

loves nature and yearns
for peace and harmony.

RED

is the leader of the birds.
He protects the eggs at all costs.

CHEF PIG

is always scheming to overthrow King Pig and become the king himself.

CORPORAL PIG

is the loyal leader of the King's army, though he is quite stupid and has no natural authority.

MINION PIGS

are the lowest of the low in Pig society, but they are happy in their place.

KING PIG

is the only pig who is allowed to eat eggs. The king's biggest secret is that he has no eggs in his treasure chamber.

JIM, JAKE & JAY

are the youngest members of the flock. They like playing pranks.

One soap bubble. Two soap bubbles. Soap bubbles continued to float over the hill until Stella appeared. "These are the best bubbles I've ever made!" Stella said happily. "This is going to be a fantastic day!"

"*Ffffw, ffffw!*" The morning was perfectly quiet but for the sound of Stella blowing bubbles. Suddenly, the silence was interrupted by heartbroken cries. Stella dropped her bubble wand and spun around.

"Help is on the way!"

Stella ran through the forest and across the meadow like a streak of pink lightning. Following the screams was easy, and she soon found what she was looking for.

It was Matilda. "Oh, woe is me. Woe is me. This is a disaster! A disaster, I tell you!" she cried.

"Stop squawking. Help is here," Stella said.

Then she noticed that the others had arrived on the scene as well. Bubbles twittered to Matilda sympathetically until Red moved him aside.

"If this is an emergency, the baby chicks need to stay out of the way."

Stella wondered if Red meant her, too. If he did, she didn't plan to listen.

Red ordered Matilda to tell him what was going on.

"Everything is ruined," Matilda moaned. "My power has been stolen."

"What do you mean?" Red snapped.

"My amulet of power is missing—my jade egg! Without it, I can't do anything."

"And this is supposed to be an emergency?" Red asked, but everyone could see that Matilda was seriously upset.

"I can help Matilda guard the eggs," Stella said. "I'm not scared and I . . ."

"Out of the question," Red snorted. "You just blow your bubbles and try to keep out of the way."

Who did that rude red rooster think he was! Stella shook with anger, a firecracker ready to explode. However, Red didn't pay her any attention.

"I'll go look for her trinket," Red announced. "Stella and Bubbles, you stay with Matilda. Is that clear?"

"Wee-wee," Bubbles replied.

Stella mumbled something like a yes, but to Bubbles she whispered, "I have other plans."

Once Red left, Stella said, "I can guess where Matilda's charm is."

Matilda just sighed, but Bubbles was clearly interested, bouncing around Stella with his eyes all lit up.

"Okay, my mighty little mandarin. You can be my traveling buddy!" Stella said. "But be warned: This trip will be dangerous."

Bubbles' enthusiasm only seemed to grow. "Weep-wee!" he shouted.

"Don't worry, Matilda. You'll have your charm back sooner than you think," Stella promised.

"First we have to stop by my secret hiding place to pick up some supplies," Stella explained to Bubbles.

Bubbles chirped in question, but Stella kept her surprise a mystery until they arrived at her hiding place.

"Check this out!" Stella said, taking out a green snout made from a hollow piece of wood and putting it over her beak.

"Yak-yak-yak!" Bubbles said in disgust. Stella laughed.

"Exactly! This is my snout mask, and I have one for you, too. Now we're off to Pig City. I'm sure they stole Matilda's charm. It just so happens that I overheard a conversation this morning . . ."

Hiding in some nearby bushes, three blue figures watched Stella and Bubbles: Blue Jim, Blue Jake, and Blue Jay.

"What are they up to?" the Blues wondered. "Whatever it is, it seems exciting. Let's follow them!"

On the way to Pig City, Stella and Bubbles hatched a plan to fool the pigs. Well, Stella planned, and Bubbles agreed with all of her ideas.

"Tricking the pigs will be easy. We'll just put the masks on and walk right through the front gate," Stella assured Bubbles.

Stella suspected it wouldn't be quite that easy, but the plan still sounded good.

At the gates of Pig City, Stella and Bubbles were stopped by two guards.

"Oink! Password!" the uglier pig demanded.

"Password," Stella replied in as gruff a voice as she could manage.

The pig accepted her reply, but the slightly less ugly pig said to his partner, "These pigs are strange. They smell funny."

"Why is your skin pink?" he asked Stella.

"Because it's fashionable, you rotten side of bacon," Stella growled.

"Really?" The pigs looked at each other. "But why are your ears so small?"

"So I don't have to listen to your grunting. We're in a hurry. King Pig is waiting for us," Stella said.

The guard pigs hesitated but allowed Stella and Bubbles through the gate. They started chatting about what other colors might be fashionable.

"I want to be pink like that, too," one of them whined.

"Yip-yip-yip," Bubbles chirped once they were inside the city.

"Shh," Stella said sternly. "There are a lot of pigs around. We can't let them discover us."

They stopped a pig passing by who looked small and easy to fool.

"Hey, friend," Stella said to the pig. "Where did we put that new egg?"

The pig laughed.

"Don't you remember, pink pig? Chef Pig has been boiling it for a while now. It's still in the pot. Can't you hear the clattering?"

Suddenly the pig stopped chuckling. He frowned.

"Why would you ask about something everybody knows? And why are you two so colorful?"

Maybe this pig wasn't as stupid as he looked.

"We're sick," she said. "Haven't you heard about the pink-orange fever that takes away your memory?"

"I haven't heard anything like that!" the pig growled. "You're up to something, I can tell. You're coming with me to talk to Corporal Pig."

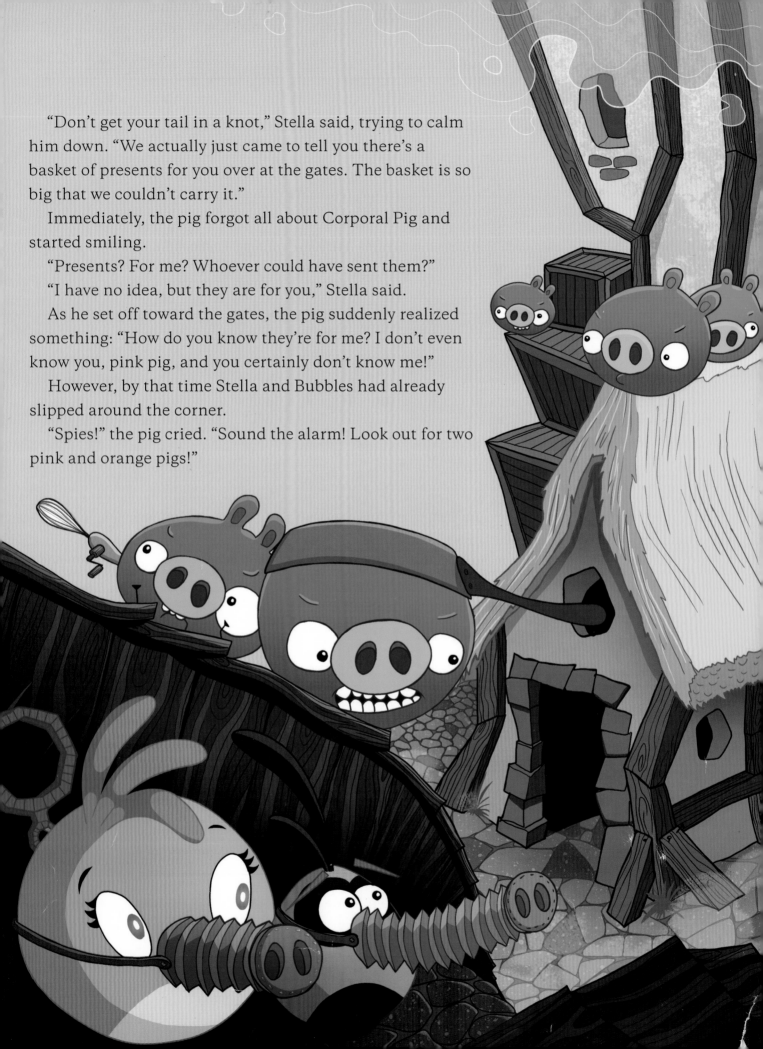

"Don't get your tail in a knot," Stella said, trying to calm him down. "We actually just came to tell you there's a basket of presents for you over at the gates. The basket is so big that we couldn't carry it."

Immediately, the pig forgot all about Corporal Pig and started smiling.

"Presents? For me? Whoever could have sent them?"

"I have no idea, but they are for you," Stella said.

As he set off toward the gates, the pig suddenly realized something: "How do you know they're for me? I don't even know you, pink pig, and you certainly don't know me!"

However, by that time Stella and Bubbles had already slipped around the corner.

"Spies!" the pig cried. "Sound the alarm! Look out for two pink and orange pigs!"

Instantly, the whole city was on the alert, with pigs running every which way and bumping into each other. One color-blind pig started accusing all the other pigs of being pink and orange, causing even more confusion.

Stella and Bubbles hid in the shadows.

"We could get caught any minute," Stella whispered. "How are we going to find Chef Pig's house?"

"Weep-weep," Bubbles whispered, nodding straight ahead. Stella turned to look. There, ahead of them, was a house shaped like a pot, its roof banging up and down as it let off steam. There was only one pig it could belong to!

Chef Pig was boiling the small green egg the pigs had found while exploring. He had to cook it for King Pig, who was already waiting impatiently. At last he would have eggs to eat!

However, Chef Pig had a problem. He had been cooking the egg for almost two days now, but it was still so hard that he couldn't get the shell to break. The egg rattled against the edges of the pot as Chef Pig stirred his concoction.

"Whoever eats eggs can be king. So says Piggy Law," Chef Pig said to himself. "And I can think of a certain chef who would make a much better king than the one we have now. Maybe I won't give this egg to King Pig after all . . ."

Chef Pig smiled at the thought. Just then, a strange noise came from outside. What was going on out there?

Stella and Bubbles were drumming on a trash can lid to get Chef Pig's attention. When the pig rushed out the door, they jumped in through the window.

The pot was bubbling on the stove.

"There's Matilda's jade egg! I'm sure of it," Stella whispered. Bubbles grabbed the ladle and started fishing the egg out of the pot, stopping to taste the broth. "Yum-yum-yum."

"No time for taste tests," Stella hissed. Bubbles dunked the ladle into the soup again and pulled out the small green egg.

"We found it!" Stella shouted in triumph. "Now Red will see who should stay out of the way."

"Weep-wee!" Bubbles chimed in as they started dancing a victory dance and wagging their feathers. But then they heard pigs yelling outside: "Lock the gates! Guards, to the walls! Search every house until you find the spies!"

Stella and Bubbles froze. They heard noises at the door. The pigs were coming!

"Out, to the gates," Stella ordered, shoving Bubbles through the window and then following. While the pigs were rushing back and forth, slamming doors and racing to their guard posts, the birds managed to run to the gates.

To her horror, Stella realized that the gates of the city were already closed. Even without any guards, the wall would have been impossible to climb. It was simply too high.

"We have to come up with something else," Stella said. But what? Pigs were everywhere, and they were all grunting furiously.

When Chef Pig noticed that his precious egg was gone, he ran outside and looked all around, sizzling with anger. The thieves couldn't have gone far. There! A flash of pink and orange! Those colors didn't belong in Pig City.

"Guards, over here!" Chef Pig roared. "We've got those miserable spies trapped."

He watched with satisfaction as the pink and orange shapes pressed against the wall as pigs approached from every direction.

"This is going to take a miracle," Stella whispered to Bubbles. "There are too many pigs. How are we going to get out of here?"

But Bubbles didn't seem worried at all. What did he have in mind?

Suddenly, Bubbles started doing something incredible—something Stella had never seen before.

Bubbles started to inflate. As he huffed and puffed, Stella began to understand his brilliant plan. She jumped on his back. Then Bubbles inflated more. And more.

It wasn't long before Bubbles was as tall as the wall. All Stella had to do was jump off of Bubbles' back and—*boing!*—she bounced over the wall as if she were jumping on a trampoline. The pigs just stood at the gate watching in amazement as Stella flew over their heads, smiling sweetly and sticking out her tongue.

Then Bubbles let out all the air and exploded into the sky like a balloon. Now it was his turn to fly over the pigs.

"Woo-hoo!" he shouted as he glided through the air and then dropped down next to Stella.

"That was a great trick," Stella said. "If only Red could have been here to see it!"

Stella wanted to hug Bubbles and let him know that he was the mightiest miracle mandarin ever. But there was no time for that. The pigs had opened the gate and were coming after Stella and Bubbles.

"We're going to have to move at record speed to get to the rocks before the pigs. We'll be able to hide there," Stella said.

"Get them!" shouted Chef Pig, bouncing along at the front of the group. He looked furious.

"Maybe you'll have to blow yourself up again and roll them flat," Stella suggested. But then she wondered, "Would that even stop all of them? They're like the waves of the sea."

Even though it felt hopeless, Stella knew she couldn't give up. Bubbles had just helped her, and now it was her turn to protect him.

The herd of pigs was rolling forward like a giant wave, but then the birds started hearing howls of pain: "Ouch! Ow! Eek!"

The pigs slowed down and then stopped completely. What was happening?

That was when Stella noticed Jim, Jake, and Jay, who were attacking the pigs with rocks. Bubbles squeaked with joy.

"We followed you," Jim said. "Then we saw that you needed help."

Stella thought Jim sounded a bit full of himself.

"No we didn't," she replied. "We were fine."

"Oh, you were, were you?" the Blues laughed.

"We would have been fine without you," Stella snapped.

"She's funny when she's angry," Jake whispered dreamily.

Once more, Stella turned toward the frustrated pigs, bouncing high in the air and sticking out her tongue.

"Serves you right, socket snouts!"

Matilda was over the moon when Stella, Bubbles, and the Blues returned her jade egg. Carefully putting it back on her necklace, she said, "I feel stronger already. Stella and Bubbles, you're my heroes! How did you figure out that the egg was in Pig City?"

Stella ruffled up her feathers in pride. "I happened to overhear a pig scouting party. They were going on about the miniature egg they had found. At the time, I thought they had just found an egg-shaped mushroom or something. It wasn't until later that I realized what it was."

Matilda praised Stella's resourcefulness and shook her feathers.

"Good. Everything is back to normal," Red grumbled.

"Can Bubbles and I guard the eggs now?" Stella asked. "We've shown that we can outsmart the pigs."

Red's reply was stern: "That was a clever trick, but you can't guard the eggs. That requires experience and raw power."

Red was the most irritating creature Stella had ever met! He clearly needed a good feather-dusting. Stella was just about to pounce when Matilda sighed.

"Actually, I'm feeling weak again."

"So you aren't better after all?" Red snapped.

Matilda winked at Stella. "I just don't have the strength to guard the eggs. At least not alone. I could use a couple of good assistants."

Red clucked his beak. "I see through your plot, Matilda, but so be it. Stella and Bubbles can help you watch the eggs, but it will be years before I let them do guard duty alone. They're just too young and thoughtless to be full-time egg guards."

Was that so? Stella would show Red who was thoughtless!

Once Red had left, Stella and Bubbles started their victory dance again. This time, Matilda danced with them.

"We get to guard the eggs!" Stella cheered.

"But not on your own," Matilda reminded them.

Stella just laughed. "I'll be guarding alone before you know it, and so will Bubbles. You'll see! We just have to get Red used to the idea."

"You won't be able to soften Red up that easily," Matilda insisted.

"We'll see about that," Stella said. "What do you say, Bubbles?"

"Weep-wee!"

The victory dance continued for a long time, and the Blues joined in. Above them all, Stella blew soap bubbles, which reflected back their happy faces and bright colors: white, orange, blue. And pink, of course!

Written by Sari Peltoniemi
Translated by Owen F. Witesman
Illustrations by Noora Katto

INSIGHT KIDS
PO Box 3088
San Rafael, CA 94912
www.insighteditions.com

 Find us on Facebook: www.facebook.com/InsightEditions
 Follow us on Twitter: @insighteditions

Translation rights arranged by Elina Ahlbäck Literary Agency.

Library of Congress Cataloging-in-Publication Data available.

ISBN: 978-1-60887-376-0

 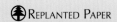

Insight Editions, in association with Roots of Peace, will plant two trees for each tree used in the manufacturing of this book. Roots of Peace is an internationally renowned humanitarian organization dedicated to eradicating land mines worldwide and converting war-torn lands into productive farms and wildlife habitats. Roots of Peace will plant two million fruit and nut trees in Afghanistan and provide farmers there with the skills and support necessary for sustainable land use.

Manufactured in China by Insight Editions

10 9 8 7 6 5 4 3 2 1

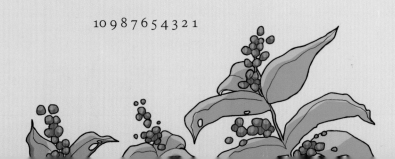